TOP OF THE PUPS

The Puppy Plan

Anna Wilson has two black cats called Ink and Jet. She was always a Cat-Type Person until she got her gorgeous black Labrador, Kenna. Now she is a Cat-AND-Dog-Type Person, and she keeps chickens and a tortoise too. She has just about enough space in her house for her husband and two children as well. They all live together in Bradford on Avon in Wiltshire. Anna has written many young-fiction titles for Macmillan Children's Books and plans to write many, many more!

Books by Anna Wilson

The Great Kitten Cake Off
I'm a Chicken, Get Me Out of Here!
Monkey Business
Monkey Madness: The Only Way Is Africa!

The Pooch Parlour series
The Poodle Problem
The Dotty Dalmatian
The Smug Pug

The Top of the Pups series
The Puppy Plan
Pup Idol
Puppy Power
Puppy Party

Kitten Kaboodle
Kitten Smitten
Kitten Cupid

And for older readers
Summer's Shadow

www.annawilson.co.uk

TOP of the PUPS

The PUPPY PLAN

Anna Wilson

Illustrated by Moira Munro

MACMILLAN CHILDREN'S BOOKS

First published 2008 by Macmillan Children's Books as *Puppy Love*

This edition published 2015 by Macmillan Children's Books
an imprint of Pan Macmillan
a division of Macmillan Publishers Limited
20 New Wharf Road, London N1 9RR
Associated companies throughout the world
www.panmacmillan.com

ISBN 978-1-4472-7611-1

1 3 5 7 9 8 6 4 2

A CIP catalogue record for this book is available from
the British Library.

Typeset by Nigel Hazle
Printed and bound by CPI Group (UK) Ltd, Croydon CR0 4YY

For David, Lucy, Tom
With love

Contents

1
How to Be Persistent

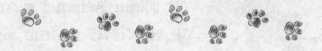

This is the story of how my wish came true. The wish that I, Summer Holly Love, have been holding close to my heart for all of my life – well, for as long as I can remember, anyway.

It's also the story of how my older sister, April Lydia Love, nearly wrecked my wish and (almost) made me wish I hadn't wished it, because of her totally weird and unforgivably embarrassing behaviour. More of that later.

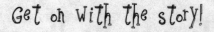

Get on with the story!

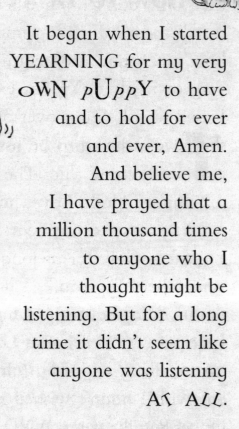

It began when I started YEARNING for my very OWN pUppY to have and to hold for ever and ever, Amen. And believe me, I have prayed that a million thousand times to anyone who I thought might be listening. But for a long time it didn't seem like anyone was listening AT ALL.

Like you're not listening to me now?

The funny thing about people not
listening to you, I have found, is that
they only don't listen when you're trying
to tell them something important, like
how much you are yearning for your
very own pUppY! For example, when
I used to ask Mum over and over again
she never seemed to be listening at all,
but always said, 'Hmm, maybe. Ask
me again when I'm not driving around
a roundabout/reversing into a blinking
tight car-parking space.'

But then whenever I had to tell her
things I'd rather not, like, 'I'm sorry
I seem to have got extra homework
again,' she was always on a totally
different wavelength altogether and heard
me vERY loUD AND ClEAR
INDEED.

3

Boy, are you long-winded

I have to say though, I am now living proof that it really pays off to be PERSISTENT, as Molly Cook, my best friend, would say. (Molly is great at using long words and then explaining them to you so that you can just NONCHALANTLY drop them into conversations to impress people when they are not expecting it.)

So, after being persistent about the puppy for the longest time ever, I got the

chance to be even more persistenter when a boy in my class called Frank

(who's OK most of the time as long as you don't sit next to him towards the end of the week because he only changes his socks on a Monday, and, like, do they start to honk by Wednesday afternoon) said that his Labrador (who has the unfortunate name of Meatball) had had pUppIES!

At last! I thought you'd never get there . . .

He brought in photos and everything. And were those puppies CUTE or what?

Oh stop, this is getting embarrassing!

Mr Elgin even let Frank stand up in class and tell us about the puppies being born, and how he'd stayed up all night to watch. And then Frank put on this kind of serious voice you hear on the radio when people are advertising things for sale and said:

Every puppy needs a good home, so if you are interested, please do not hesitate to contact me and arrange an appointment.

But remember, kids:
a Puppy is for Life,
Not Just for Christmas.

Which was a daft thing to say, as we'd only just had Easter. I even still had a stash of mini eggs left in my secret place under my bed behind my Celebrity Club folder, next to my torch.

At that point Mr Elgin said, 'Thank you, Frank, that will do. Go back to your place, please.' So Frank did.

After that I really couldn't concentrate on any lessons. I was just watching the clock on the wall, which definitely moves a lot slower than the one at home, and

thinking that if I thought hard enough
the hands would move faster and it
would be break time quicker.

It didn't work, but at last someone
rang the bell for break and we all made a
beeline for the playground. I
normally just go straight into the corner
with Molly and we do our Celebrity
Club, but today I had to have a Very
Important Appointment with Frank to
discuss the Puppy Situation. So that's why
I made the beeline.

Frank was kicking a ball around
as usual, so when I said, 'Frank, about
those puppies,' he didn't hear me.
Honestly, sometimes I just think I'm
INVISIBLE. So I made my beeline
right in front of him and
did a bit of nifty footwork
and got the ball off him

and passed it skilfully to one of his smelly
mates.

'Oi!' said Frank.

'Summer, actually,' I said, and I
folded my arms like Mum does when you
know she means business.

'What?' said Frank. Boys really are
the thickest sandwich in the picnic basket
sometimes. I tried again.

'I said, "About those puppies."'

'No, you didn't,' said Frank. 'You
said, "Summer actually."'

He's right, you did.

I raised my eyebrows and sighed in a
particularly dramatical manner and said,
'That's my name.'

'What are you on about?' said Frank.

It was then that I knew I had to

use my most Mum-like tone to get his attention. 'I want to talk to you about your puppies, Frank Gritter.'

'You'll have to make an appointment,' he said importantly and tried to get past me, back to his football-playing mates.

'I am making an appointment right now,' I said. This is how to be truly persistent, I thought.

Frank sighed and said, 'Come round after tea — but my mum says anyone interested has to have Parental Consent.'

I wasn't sure what Parental Consent was, but I thought that it must be something to do with parents, and that I could probably get anything I wanted now that I was in such a persistent frame of mood.

'OK,' I said, and stepped to one side

so that Frank could kick a ball around again and make his socks even more sweatier. I made a mental reminder not to stand too close to him at his house that night.

Did someone mention socky-whiff?
Mmmm, my favourite!

2

How to Get Parental Consent

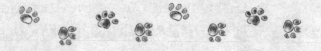

I stared at those clock hands for the rest of the day, which meant I didn't get much out of the history lesson about the Victorians that we had in the afternoon, but to be totally honest I don't ever get much out of the history lessons we have about the Victorians. I know that the Victorians had a queen called Queen Victoria, which I always thought was quite clever of them, and I know that they invented penny-farthing bicycles, but frankly what use were they? I don't know anyone today who has even the slightest use for a penny-farthing bicycle. And even in the Victorian olden times only people with the most UNFEASIBLY long legs must have been able to ride them. So I don't get much out of the Victorians, personally. Especially when I'm thinking about how to get Parental Consent so that I can at last get my very own pUppY.

That's right – focus, kid, focus.

Someone in the school did finally decide to ring the bell for the end of the day (one day I will find out who this person is and

13

have a word with them to see if they can
ring it earlier, as all this waiting around for
the bell to ring is very tiring), so, without
waiting for Molly like I normally do, I
ran all the way home. And on the way
I started practising my very-well-planned
conversation that I'd made up in my head
during the history lesson. It went something
like this:

'Hello, Mum. That's a lovely dress
you're wearing. Oh, and your hair is
beautiful today. Did you
know that my friends
think you are the most
nicest-looking mum of
all the mums?'

At this point
Mum would
smile and
say, 'How lovely,

Summer. And may I say that you are
looking most gorgeous today yourself?'

Then I would say, 'Mum, can I get you
anything? Let me make you a cup of
tea. You must have had a hard
day.'

And I would lead her to a chair and sit
her down and fetch some of those lemony
biscuits which she loves but which she is
always trying not to eat as they are 'so
bad for the figure'. And then I'd make her

a cup of tea while chatting in a friendly way about my day at school, which she always wants me to do, but which I never do because I'm always in a hurry to watch *Seeing Stars* on telly.

I have to say a bit about this show, because it is truly the most inspirationalist of shows I have ever seen on The Box (as Mum likes to call the telly, in that old-fashioned way of hers). It is a show which is a contest for people to become Celebrities, which is of course what my biggest AMBITION is. And because Molly is my best friend, it is her ambition too.

To enter this show it doesn't even matter what your talent is, you just have to have one. So you could be a brilliant singer, or a top dancer or a mega-magician or even just be really good at telling jokes. Then you get

up on stage in front of what is called a Panel
of Judges (although why it is called this I
have no idea, as they are just people sitting
behind a desk, and there is no panelling in
sight at all) and you PERFORM.

If the person is very good, the judges are
kind and lovely and say wonderful things
about how great the performance is. If the
person is bad, they say horrible things that
I wouldn't even say to someone like Frank
Gritter. They say, 'That was truly the worst
dance I have ever had to sit through. You
looked like a sack of potatoes on the back
of a lorry driving down a bumpy road, and
your dress looks like it's covered in cat sick,'
or something like that. The person then has
to try very hard not to cry because it is
embarrassing on telly if you cry. (Unless you
are supposed to because you are acting in a
dramatical drama of some kind.)

Anyway, once the judges have said who they like best, which is the bit which Molly says is called 'Delivering the VERDICT', we, the audience at home, get to vote BY pHONING THE ACTUAL STUDIO! Except I never can as Mum says the phone bill would go through the roof if I did. (And how on earth a phone bill is able to rocket through bricks and tiles etc., I do not know. Mum does say weird things.)

Anyway, because I cannot vote, Molly and I decided to set up our own Celebrity Club instead. And we do it after school whenever we can, usually underneath my bed which is one of those ones on a platform where you have a desk under it. Molly and I are going to be famous with our Celebrity Club and we'll be on telly with our own show just like the people on *Seeing Stars*. One day.

How to Get Parental Consent

But unfortunately for me, I was not a famous celebrity on the day in question, which was the day I was trying to get Mum to let me have a puppy. So instead of using my powers of celebrity, I had to use my powers of persuasion to get Mum to listen to me.

To go back to my very-well-planned conversation in my head, after telling Mum what a YUMMY MUMMY she was, the next thing I thought I would say in my friendly chatty manner was:

'A very interesting thing happened this morning at school, actually, because my charming friend, Frank Gritter, told us that his Labrador has had pUppIES and that we are all most welcome to come and see them after tea at his house. As long as we have Parental Consent.'

And then Mum would answer . . .

★

'Summer! What on earth have you got down your shirt?'

Mum had been spying on me running down the road and I had not noticed because my head was full of my very-well-planned conversational ideas. She had come out of the house and stopped me in mid-tracks. I screeched to a halt like people in cartoons do whenever they see a seriously bad Baddie and blurted out:

'Hello, Mum. That's a lovely skirt/dress/T-shirt you're wearing—' Whoops. Forgot to delete as applicable.

 Not your smartest move, I have to say . . .

'What?' She closed her eyes and shook her head. She always does this when I say something she considers to be silly. She sighed, gave me a kiss, then turned to go into the house and I followed her down the hall.

I decided to try out my very-well-planned conversation, so I went into the kitchen and threw my bag and pakamac down by the radiator, which is my usual place for putting my things as I can always find them then.

Mum sighed noisily and went to pick up my bag but I put my hand on her arm in a gentle and concerned fashion and said, 'Come and sit down and I'll make you a nice cup of tea. You must have had a hard day.'

Mum's eyes did something very strange then. They looked as if they were going

21

to pop out of her head, and I'm sure she actually stopped breathing. But she did go and sit down. Good thing really. If she had actually stopped breathing in true life she might have fainted, and I couldn't let that happen before I had asked her about the pUppIES.

Too right, sister!

I made a lovely cup of tea and got the lemony biscuits.

Mum narrowed her eyes at the biscuits. 'What are you up to, Summer?' she said in a suspicious manner. 'Oh, put those biscuits away – they are so bad for the figure.'

She ate three while I started to tell her in a pleasant and chatty way about my day and how Molly and I had played with Rosie Chubb in first break, but then

How to Get Parental Consent

Rosie Chubb had got in a mood with
us because we wouldn't tell her about
our club, so she poked a pencil in
Molly's arm and Molly had to go
to the Welfare Room to see whether
or not we would have to call an
ambulance. I had personally thought
an ambulance would definitely be needed,
as I had seen on telly that you could get
lead poisoning if lead got in your skin or
blood or something. Molly had said she
was positive she would need a blood test to
check her Heemi-Goblins Level. At least, I
thought that's what she said, but she was
doing that hiccuping crying she does when
she's really panicky so I hadn't been able
to hear very well what she was saying.
(Actually, she can't have said that, as how
can there be goblins in your blood?)

But the nurse said we were Making

a Fuss and that
pencils don't have
real lead in any
more. So at lunch
we decided to
break up with
Rosie Chubb

because she couldn't be our friend if she was
going to stick pencils in us that weren't even
real lead, and anyway by that time a more
interesting thing had happened which was,
'. . . my charming friend Frank telling us
about his dog's puppies—'

Mum choked a bit on the last crumbs of
her third lemony biscuit and said in a rather
strangled voice, 'Oh no!'

'Are you all right?' I asked in my
most anxious and worried tone. Maybe
the biscuits had started to upset her figure.
'Should I call a doctor?'

'NO!' Mum bellowed, coughing and spluttering. 'I should have known you were up to something.'

'Me?' I said, pointing at my chest and making my eyes do that wide innocent thing people do on telly when they can't believe someone is saying that they've done something they very much obviously have.

'Yes, YOU, young lady. You're trying yet again to get me to agree to having a dog. Well, I won't. Ever.'

Wow, she's one tough lady.

I felt a little tiny-weeny bit cross at this. That's the last time I make tea and get out the lemony biscuits and chat about my day, I thought. But then I remembered that I was supposed to be being persistent and getting Parental Consent, so instead of sulking and saying, 'It's not fair,' I said in my grown-up-discussion voice, 'I don't really understand why you are so unkeen on the idea.'

'Because it would end up being *my* dog,' she said.

I'm sure Mum and I speak a different language most of the time: I was asking for my very *own* puppy, so in what way would it end up being *Mum's* dog? So I asked her, 'Excuse me, Mum, but in what way would it end up being *your* dog?'

'In the way that *I* would be the one clearing up after its mess, *I* would be the one taking it for walks and *I* would be the one taking it to the vet,' Mum said in, I have to say, a quite unpleasant tone of talking.

'But you wouldn't!' I protested. 'I'm totally brilliant at going for walks and clearing up messes.'

How to Get Parental Consent

'Huh!' Mum did a half-snort and a grunt. Not very attractive, in my opinion.

You should hear yourself sometimes, kiddo . . .

'Listen,' I said trying to sound soothing and sensible. 'I *promise* I would take it out for a walk every day before school. And I'd get one of those super-duper pooper-scooper things to clear up any mess it makes,' I said, smiling like an angel.

'Summer,' she said in her most DECISIVE and scariest way, 'I remember you saying similar things about the stick insects, before they mysteriously disappeared. In fact, whatever happened to them . . . ?'

Here we go yet again, I thought wearily. But I tried not to look wearily and kept the angelical smile on my face. It was beginning to feel a bit stiff. (By the way, I'm sure I never promised to take the stick insects for a walk every day.)

'And what about the cats?' she was still wittering on. 'Who feeds them every day and picks up all the dead mice and birds they bring in through the cat flap?'

'You do,' I admitted, smiling carefully, 'but I never wanted the cats anyway.'

I probably shouldn't have said that last bit, but it was totally true. *Mum* had always wanted cats. I think she thought that if she got cats then I'd forget all about how much I yearned for a *pUppY*. But the thing is, Cheese and Toast're not that much fun now they're not kittens. They just sleep all day and go out all night. (Sometimes I actually wish I was a cat. I would have a nice life, and I certainly wouldn't have to learn my seven times table.) Besides, they are not very cuddly and the only lap they'll sit on is Mum's.

 Yup. They're dull, dull dull.

'Oh, come on, Mum, pur-*leeese*!' I had given up on the smile by now and was doing that thing when you've got your hands between your legs as if you desperately need to go to the loo and my eyes were tight shut and I was doing what I think is called a Grimace, in other words my mouth was stretched in an expression of complete AGONY and I was showing all my teeth. I was also whining. I think I looked like what Molly calls an Utter Nutter, I'm embarrassed to say. '*Please* give me Parental Consent and come with me to Frank's and have a look at them.'

'Oh, anything to stop you pulling those bizarre faces,' she said grudgingly. And I'm sure she almost smiled.

I could feel my eyes going shiny and I felt BUBBLY WITH EXCITEMENT. I jumped up to give her a hug and disastrously knocked her teacup flying. This was not a good move and totally definitely not part of my very-well-planned conversation.

How to Get Parental Consent

She threw a cloth at me and cried,
'Before we go anywhere, you'd better prove
how good you are at clearing up messes!'

The thing about mums is, they always get
the last word.

3

How to Be Persuasive

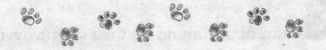

I chewed my nails all the way to Frank's. I had promised myself never to chew my nails again because I know it is not what celebrity people do, and Molly says that if we are going to Get Anywhere with our Celebrity Club, we must not bite our nails any more. So I had painted them with this shiny stuff which I thought looked Glam and Gorgeous like the real nail varnish my sister, April, wears but it actually tastes Grim with a capital G! There is one problem I have found though. If you are truly stressed and anxious about something, you will always find a way to stop thinking about the Grim taste and you will always bite your nails anyway. So that's what I was doing on the way to Frank's house.

I just kept thinking and turning it over in my head: 'What if the whole class has already been there and all the puppies have gone? What if Frank laughs at me and says, 'Ha ha! You are too late, Summer Holly Love!' and what if there's not much room in the room and I have to stand too close to him and try not to be sick because of the smell of his socks? Because if I was sick because of the smell of his socks, he might be angry and not let me take one of the puppies. And what if Mum just takes one look at the puppies and says, 'NO WAY HO-ZAY,' like they do in films and then Frank laughs and says, 'I told you you needed Parental Consent!'

33

'Does Frank's mother know we are coming to look at these puppies?' Mum asked, breaking her way into my most anxious thoughts.

Why do mums always worry about other mums knowing whether you are coming round or not? Molly's mum, Mrs Cook, is always happy to see me whenever I turn up and she says, 'It's nice to see you girls playing together,' and she always gives us flapjacks with apricots in, which she knows are my favourite.

I just shrugged and said, 'Frank said to come round.'

Mum sighed and muttered something about 'getting this over and done with'.

I rang the bell and we waited. I thought we might hear yapping or barking as Frank said there were eight puppies, but there was not a sound of a dog at all.

How to Be Persuasive

Frank opened the door and Mum took a step back. The sock smell was particularly of a whiffy nature.

Yum!

I held my breath and tried to speak quickly so that I wouldn't have to breathe in the honking smell.

'Hello, we are here because I have got Parental Consent to have an appointment with you about the puppies.'

Frank grinned and led us into his house. His mum was in the kitchen. I was really very surprised to see that she was quite clean and normal-looking. She did not smell of socks at all. The kitchen was even tidier than our own, in actual fact.

Mum had got her 'Isn't this nice? I'm ever so delighted to be here' smile on. The

35

mums started a chat about school and how lovely it was that they had children in Year Four now and what a difference it made.

I didn't know how much of a difference it could make to anyone what year we were in, but mums are always saying things like this. Molly says she thinks it's all a secret language that only mums understand. They say these things to each other that we think are dull and make no sense, but then they always seem to have picked up all kinds of information that we don't want them to have about our lives. And they always say they got it from someone else's mum. Maybe the government gives you a secret handbook when you become a mum that tells you the language so you can learn it in time for your children to start school. Governments do that kind of thing. I've seen it on telly.

Anyway, Frank did a circly thing with his eyes and beckoned to me to follow him. He obviously thought that mum-conversations are totally baffling and dull too. We went out of the kitchen into the room where the washing machine was. I hoped he wasn't going to ask me to wash his socks while I was there.

'Why are we in here?' I asked. 'I thought you were going to show me the puppies.'

'They're in here, stupid,' said Frank. He obviously does not know that to be a truly successful sales-person you have to be charming and polite. Not rude and smelly.

He pointed to a large box in the corner of the room. I heard a small snuffling noise and rushed over to have a look. I could *not* believe what my eyes were telling me. On the far side of the box, snuggled up against Meatball, were the tiniest, cutest, squidgiest *p*U*pp*IES ever in the whole world!

We pups aim to please . . .

'Why have they all got their eyes closed?' I asked Frank, as I suddenly felt a little bit confused.

'Don't you even know *that*?' Frank asked in his huffy, girls-are-the-stupidest voice.

I felt my face going a bit red and hot which I don't like as it doesn't go extremely

well with the colour of my hair which is
what I like to call auburn, but my sister,
April, calls ginger.

'Well, they're very much obviously not
asleep, are they?' I said importantly. 'I can
see with my own eyes that they are moving
around – unless they are sleepwalking?'
I asked, feeling pleased with myself for
coming up with this brilliant explanation.

'Duh, stupid – they *can't* open their eyes,'
he said with what can only be described
as a very smug, know-it-all grin on his
unattractive features.

I put my hands on my hips to show
that I was not a girl to be messed with
or talked to in that manner. 'In that case,
Frank Gritter, you have broken the Sales
and Tradespersons Description Act,' I said
importantly. (Luckily I knew about this
because Molly told me that if you are

selling something you have to be truthful about all the details of what precisely you are getting, otherwise the government can put you in prison.) 'Who wants a puppy who can't open its eyes?'

'Oh, shut up,' said Frank. 'These little guys can't open their eyes because they are not even two weeks old. You would know this if you had been listening to what I said this morning. They are still being weaned. They should open their eyes any day now. That's why you can't take one home yet, even if you definitely want one and have definitely got Parental Consent. You can have one at seven or eight weeks. They'll be ready at half-term actually.'

I made a mental reminder to go and look up what 'weaned' meant. And also to check in a book whether or not Frank was telling the truth about the puppies not being

able to open their eyes yet. I did not want
to be sold a dog who could not fetch a stick
or a ball. How would I teach it tricks if it
could not see? I could not be a Responsible
Dog-Owner-Type person if I could not
train my dog. Anyway, I certainly was not
going to ask Frank about my Concerns, as
it would show that I was a tiny bit ignorant
of dog-type Issues, and then he might not
think I would be a suitable owner of a
pUppY.

Well, the thought did cross
my mind . . .

'Can I hold one?' I asked.

He reached into the box and picked up
one of the puppies. 'It's a girl,' he said.
A golden girl.

Frank put her into my arms. I could

41

almost have held her in one hand only.
And I nearly squealed when I touched her.
She was the MOST ABSOLUTELY
SOFTEST and VELVETEST thing you
have ever imagined. And she made small
grunty piggy noises that made me want

to squeal even more. But I didn't want to frighten her, so I just kept the squeals inside and gently stroked her.

That was when Mum and Mrs Gritter came in.

'So here's the whelping box,' said Mrs Gritter.

'Whelping': another word I absolutely had to remember to look up later.

'As I said, the puppies can't leave their mother yet, but if you want to put your name down for one, we can arrange for you to come back in a few weeks.'

I looked up at Mum, all ready to be most *p*ERSUASI*v*E AND *p*ERSIS*t*EN*t*. I had decided I wanted the puppy I was holding more than even I wanted to be the winner on *Seeing Stars*, and I was most determined to let Mum know this. But I didn't have to.

Mum looked at me holding Honey
(that's what I knew I had to call her)
and opened her mouth to say something
like, 'We'll let you know,' which is her
usual way of telling people that she's not
interested. Then Honey stretched in my
arms and sort of yawned in a very definitely
cute kind of way.

Thanks, I thought so too!

Then Mum's face went a funny blotchy red.
She closed her mouth.
Then she opened it again.
Then she raised her eyebrows, sighed
loudly and finally said:

How to Be Persuasive

'Isn't she gorgeous?'

I think in the end Honey was more
persuasive herself than I could ever have
possibly been on my own.

You said it, girl!

4
How to Be Prepared

So that was it – Mum couldn't go back on her word now. I was SO OVER THE MOON WITH GLEE AND HAPPINESS that I called Molly and told her about it straight away. She was OVER THE MOON too and said Honey could be an Honourable Member of our Celebrity Club, because lots of famous people have famous pets. Especially dogs, which they carry under their arm when they go shopping. (Although that would be a difficult thing to do with a fully grown-up Labrador.)

How to Be Prepared

Then, because I was still hyper-excitable, as soon as my sister April came home I very speedily filled her in on all the details too. April is older than me — twenty-two or some other ancient age — and works in town for an office of people who are lawyers and they are called Stingy and Gross. Apparently lawyers are always called something like Stingy and Gross. Never Mr Stingy and Ms Gross, just Stingy and Gross. Molly says it's so you know they are lawyers and not normal human beings.

(Molly and I don't want to work in town when we are older, because when we're older we're going to be famous, of course, and go on telly about our Celebrity

Club and tell everyone how we shot to fame
in an important and glamorous manner
by winning all the votes in *Seeing Stars*. So
probably then we'll be so famous we won't
have to live at home with our mums any
more like my sister April does; we'll live in a
pent-flat suite, I expect.)

'April, we're getting a pUppY!' I
screamed. This was how I very speedily
filled her in on all the details.

'Typical,' she said, with an older-sister
SOPHISTICATED sigh. 'I start life in the
working world, and *you* get a puppy.'

She says that about everything. When
we got the new big flat telly with all the
different channels she said, 'Typical. I start
life in the working world and *you* get a
digital plasma telly,' and when we went to
Spain for a holiday last year without her
because she said she wouldn't be seen dead

on holiday with her 'baby sister', she said, 'Typical. I start life in the working world and *you* go to Spain.' What does she expect? Life doesn't stop because April Love's Started Life in the Working World. That's what Mum says, and I agree.

The thing is, it probably is a bit unfair, because I know that April wanted a puppy when she was still at school, but Mum always put her foot down about it. But then April probably didn't ever have a friend at school whose dog had just had puppies so that she could take Mum to see them. In fact, I don't know if April had any friends at all at school anyway.

Ouch! You're Bad!

When April had stopped doing her sophisticated sighing she said she would like to take me shopping at the weekend to get some stuff for Honey. I was actually quite shocked by how really kind and helpful this was, as April is not usually that interested in doing things with me.

But when I told Mum she laughed and said, 'April's such a shopaholic she'd go shopping for bags of mud if that was all there was left on the planet.'

As I have already explained, Mum is well known for saying the weirdest things.

Bags of mud sound good to me!

On the way back from Frank's house the night before, I had kept on thanking Mum over and over again for saying yes to having Honey. She had smiled, but I could tell she was wondering why on earth she *had* said yes, because she put on a sort of stern face and said, 'I haven't forgotten your part of the bargain, Summer. You are going to help out with this animal. I don't want to end up doing all the work, even if I do think Honey's sweet.'

Mrs Cook once told me that when there is Tension in the Air, people often DE-FUSE THE TENSION by telling a joke. I thought it would be a good idea to have a go at doing this myself.

'You are so funny, Mum!' I said.

'Eh?' said Mum.

'"Honey's sweet!" Haha! Geddit?'

Mum groaned. But I think at least the Tension was now De-Fused, as she didn't say any more about how

much hard work it would be to have
Honey.

Hard Work? Me?

Anyway, she was right, I had
promised to help. So before the weekend
I thought I'd better Be Prepared for the
shopping trip and find out about exactly
all the special equipment a new puppy
needs.

I asked Molly the next day at school. I
didn't want to ask Frank as it was becoming
clear he was such an annoyingly know-it-
all dog-owner type, and anyway, I wanted
to steer clear, as it was Friday so the sock
aroma would be at its peak.

Molly and I were both already big fans
of the telly programme about training your
dog called *Love Me, Love My Dog*, which is

presented by a very scary-looking woman
who dresses from her top to her toes in
black shiny leather. Her name is Monica
Sitstill. She speaks in a teachery voice and
is always telling off bad owners for not
training their dogs properly. It is a funny
programme to watch, until you start to
think that you could end up being one of
those bad owners who can't train their dogs,
and then it doesn't seem quite so Amusing.
I would not like Monica Sitstill to come to
my house and talk in that teachery way to
me.

You and me Both . . .

'Monica Sitstill has written a book which
is all based on her programme, you know,'
said Molly. Molly knows everything about
everyone who's famous. That's why she

Celebrity Club

started the Celebrity Club in the very first place.

I gasped. '*Has* she? Then I must get it. It will tell me how to Be Prepared for my new vERY oWN pUppY and how to train her.'

'Indeed,' agreed Molly. 'Let's go to the library at lunchtime and get a copy, then we can start Making A List.'

Molly loves making lists. She says that it is the only way in life that a girl can be EFFORTLESSLY EFFICIENT. And it's what famous people do. That's why they never miss a party and always remember never to wear the same dress more than once at any one Celebrity Event.

So we went to the library and got a copy of the book, which was also called

Love Me, Love My Dog. It had a picture on the front of Monica Sitstill in a black leather outfit as usual and she was pointing out of the cover as if she was pointing at me, which I did find rather scary, and there was a huge dog sitting at her feet and gazing up at her in an adoring manner. The photo proved that she is obviously a very good trainer of dogs indeed if she can train a dog that big.

This was the list we made:

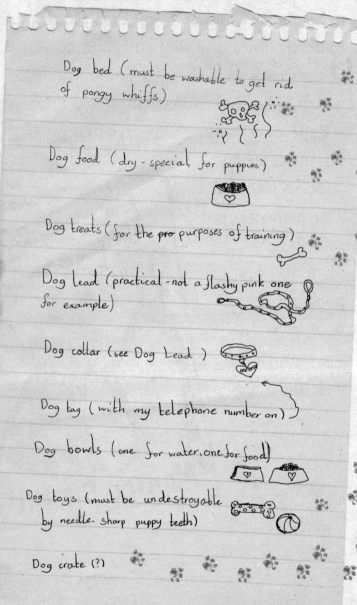

Dog bed (must be washable to get rid of pongy whiffs)

Dog food (dry - special for puppies)

Dog treats (for the ~~pro~~ purposes of training)

Dog lead (practical - not a flashy pink one for example)

Dog collar (see Dog Lead)

Dog tag (with my telephone number on)

Dog bowls (one for water, one for food)

Dog toys (must be undestroyable by needle-sharp puppy teeth)

Dog crate (?)

Pongy whiffs – YUM!

Sounds . . . er . . . mouthwatering
(NOT!) . . .

Now we're talking! (But what
is this 'training'?)

TOYS! TOYS! TOYS!

? ? ?!!!

A dog crate was a very expensive thing, and I didn't know what Mum would think about this, so I made a mental reminder to ask her before I gave April the list on Saturday and let her Run Riot with Mum's credit card. Apparently April is always Running Riot with Mum's credit card, given half the chance.

When Mum says this I always get a very strange and funny picture in my head of April snatching Mum's card and sprinting off down the street like an Olympic-style athlete, shouting loudly at the top of her head and throwing bottles and things at police officers. I'm sure that's what a riot

is, because it's what you see on the news
sometimes, but I don't think April would
really Run Riot like this as it would mess up
her long blonde straight hair.

When we had finished the list I asked
Molly if she would like to come shopping
with me and
April, and she
said, 'Do the
stars shine at
night?'

Which is
Molly's way of
saying, 'You
betcha.'

In other
words – yes.

5

How to Use Your Initiative

The weeks between seeing Honey for the first time and finally bringing her home to live with me for ever and ever were the longest weeks I have had to live through in my whole long life. I truly honestly do not know how I survived. But Molly helped me through it by phoning and coming round lots

Honey

Honey

Honey

Honey

Honey

and lots to talk about Honey and
sort out the things we had
bought for her and get the
house ready.

Honey

Honey

Molly and I read the *Love Me, Love My Dog* book about a million thousand times until I could actually quote chunks of it off by heart. I learned that 'weaning' is when the puppy starts to eat proper puppy food and stops having so much of its mother's own milk, and that a 'whelping box' is where the puppies are born and stay until their eyes have opened and they can walk. Mum started off being ever so impressed by my instant recall of all dog-related facts and figures, but I think in the end I might have annoyed her ever so slightly.

You don't say . . .

'Summer – that's enough! I know you have to de-worm a puppy dog every four weeks, I know they can't be left on their own for more than an hour to start with, and I know that I'm beginning to seriously blinking regret saying you could blinking have the blinking animal in the first blinking place!'

Hmm. Mum was getting a bit stressed and anxious about what Life With Honey was going to be like, so I did my best to calm her and reassure her that I knew what I was doing and it would all be all right in the end.

The night before we had arranged to go and collect Honey, April came home early for tea. She always seems to arrive home early when it's lasagne, even if Mum doesn't

tell her that's what we're
having. I think she's got
special lasagne-radar-
smell-o-vision and smells it
across town before it's even in the oven.

A little something we have
in common!

'A friend of mine knows someone who
works at the new vets' surgery in town,' she
told me.

'I know,' I said. 'You told me
that when we went shopping. And you
mentioned it quite a few several times last
night.'

April seemed to be very keen on getting
Honey registered with this new vet in town.
I had thought her only interest was going to
be in shopping for all manner of dog-type

equipment, especially as she is always telling me that she is far too busy at work in her office to do anything other than really important things like go shopping.

'That'll be useful,' said Mum.

'Don't we have a vet already for the cats?' I asked. I admit that I would not necessarily have known this, as I've never really got involved with Cheese or Toast's medical requirements.

'What would you know? You've never got involved with Cheese or Toast's medical requirements,' said Mum.

Cheese and Toast were both sitting at my feet and chose this moment to start purring loudly, as if they agreed with Mum.

How to Use Your Initiative

I tried to imagine what Honey would have to say . . .

In the end I couldn't think of an Appropriate Response to Mum's cutting and sarcastic remarks and instead I concentrated on getting the crispy edge of the lasagne before April could dive in and hack off her usual unfairly huge share.

'If you really are interested, Summer,' Mum continued, 'the cats have not been to the vet that much.' (Well, no wonder I didn't know about their medical requirements then!) 'They've only been for their booster jabs once a year, but since they last went, the old surgery has closed down. I've been meaning to register them with the new one, but I'm just too busy. And I'm about to get busier with Honey arriving –'

The cats purred even louder. I wondered if they knew who Honey was.

Hey, everyone around here knows about me!

I cut in quickly in a tactful manner to stop Mum starting up on an Anti-Puppy Rant. The closer we got to Honey's arrival, the more Mum was getting more stressed and anxious, and I didn't want her to suddenly change her mind about getting Honey.

'If you have the phone number, April, I'll call the vet and make an appointment to register her as soon as possible,' I offered in a very Responsible Dog-Owner way.

April blushed, which I thought at the time was a weird and strange thing to do when discussing registering a puppy with the vet. 'It's OK,' she said. 'I've already done that.'

Mum dropped her knife and fork on to her plate very dramatically and let her jaw drop, which was a bit disgusting as she still had bits of lasagne in her mouth which I could see in detail as I was sitting opposite her. She should listen to her own advice which she always gives to me on a regular basis about keeping my mouth shut while eating.

'I think I'm going to faint!' she said, being even more over-dramatical. 'Could it be? Yes – I think both daughters are actually using their initiative and being *helpful* for the first time in living memory. Actually, I must be dreaming.' And she pinched herself to check whether or not she was really awake.

And she thinks April and I are behaving strangely?

6

How to Welcome
Your Puppy

At last it was the half-term holiday and time to get Honey and bring her home to live with ME! Of course I did not sleep an entire wink the whole of the night before the BIG DAY. When I could at last see light peeping through the curtains in my room I got dressed as quietly as a very small mouse and thought I would start the day off with an exceptionally good deed, i.e. Make Breakfast. So I crept downstairs and started to make toast and get the mugs and plates out. I also moved the dog crate which we had finally bought for Honey. I thought it would be more cosier and comfier nearer the window and out of the way of draughts from the back door. I probably didn't do this particular thing as quietly as a very small mouse, because very small mice can't move large dog crates.

'What on earth are you doing, Summer?' It was Mum, looking, if I may say, quite unglamorous and disorganized, considering what an important day it was for us all.

'I'm making a special breakfast and tidying up the kitchen!' I announced proudly.

'It's half past six,

Summer, on a Saturday morning!' Mum wailed in a WOEBEGONE fashion. (I like the word 'woebegone'. Molly told me it means 'suffering or unhappy', which is exactly how Mum looked at this moment in time.)

'Well, Frank said we could come early, and I know Molly will be up bright-eyed and bushy-tailed — or maybe I'm getting her confused with Honey, ho ho!' I tried Joking to De-Fuse the Tension again. I don't think I'm all that good at it.

You might have a point there.

Mum groaned loudly and stomped back upstairs to bed.

Oh well, more toast for me, I thought, and went to watch a recording of an episode of *Seeing Stars* (which I had missed due to having to do homework or something else equally dull and unimportant) while Mum had a bit of a lie-in. I didn't seem to have woken April, but then, as Mum says, 'April wouldn't get up early on a Saturday morning even if a famous celeb was waiting outside to take her on a date,' which is obviously a ridiculous thing to say, as a famous celeb is hardly likely to take any interest whatsoever in my grumpy sister when he has got a whole range of Hollywood babes to choose from to go on a date with. And anyway, if a celeb was waiting outside, April *would* be out of bed and downstairs faster than it takes to blink very quickly, so Mum is just altogether wrong.

We *finally* got to Frank's to find Molly waiting for us. Mum looked a bit better now. She'd made an effort to put on some make-up, which I think made her look a little less tired-looking, but I noticed her socks were odd colours. One was blue and one was red. I tried not to look at them again in case I drew anyone else's attention to them. It would have been far too embarrassing. At least she wasn't wearing her fluffy slippers, thank goodness. She did once forget to take them off when she drove me to school one morning when we were late, and all my friends saw her and I nearly died right there on the spot. Luckily I think everyone was too excitable about the puppies this morning to notice odd socks.

We'd brought the car round to get Honey, even though Frank's house is only a few streets away. We didn't want to carry her all the way home in case she was wriggly and I dropped her.

On the way home I held her on my lap and she made loads of whiny noises that made me feel sad.

What do you expect? You smell weird, and the NOISE...

Frank had warned me about this.

'She will probably cry a bit, tonight especially,' he had said, 'but you must be firm with her.'

'What do you mean?' I asked. When Mum is firm with me I don't get any pocket money for a week, and I certainly am not allowed to watch *Seeing Stars*.

'I mean,' said Frank, in a voice which he probably thought was patient, but which was actually quite rude, 'that you mustn't go and see her in the night if she cries. You must leave her and then she'll learn to be OK on her own. That's what we did with Meatball.'

(I would cry all night if I'd been christened 'Meatball'.)

Mum looked more than a little bit concerned at this point. 'How loudly will she cry?' she asked, crumpling her forehead in a worried way.

Mrs Gritter smiled and said, 'All I can say is, buy yourselves some earplugs just in case.'

I thought that it would be a good idea to leave at this point, in case Frank or Mrs Gritter said anything else completely insensitively that might put Mum off letting me take Honey home. Luckily Honey was still looking very cute and cuddly and so Mum's face went all soft and gooey again when she looked at her.

I can't help it – Cute's my middle name!

When we got to my house Molly got out of the car first, and I passed Honey to her as I didn't want to drop her while I climbed out.

Frank had also given us some tiny brown dog-biscuity food that we had to feed to Honey three times a day. I went and put it on a shelf in the kitchen.

'What do we do now?' Mum asked.

April was hopping from foot to foot in a quite impatient and strange way. I thought maybe she needed to go for a pee. That reminded me of the very important thing I had learned from the *Love Me, Love My Dog* book about what to do when the puppy first comes home.

'We have to show Honey where she's allowed to go to the loo,' I said, feeling very important and responsible. 'I shall take her down to the bottom of the garden.'

I carried the warm, snuffly bundle, which was MY WISH COME TRUE, down the garden to our apple tree and said, feeling very proud and bubbly and almost like I might cry all at the same time, 'Empty!' This is the command that Monica Sitstill says you must use to tell your dog when to go to the loo.

Honey just sat there looking extremely small and tiny, like a little golden bear. She put her head on one side like she was really trying to understand me, but it was quite obvious that no one had told her what the word 'Empty' meant.

Sorry, no idea what you're on about.

I sighed and picked her up again and carried her into the kitchen. I put her down on the floor while I made sure that her dog crate was nice and cosily comfy. I was just gently and lovingly arranging her toys and blanket when Mum screamed.

It seemed Honey had finally worked out what 'Empty' meant.

'Argh! Summer, I thought you'd just taken her outside to do a pee!' Mum shrieked as a puddle spread over the kitchen floor.

How most irritating, I thought, as I stood and watched the wetness run down the line in between the kitchen tiles.

'Don't just stand there!' Mum bellowed. 'Get a cloth, get a mop, get some paper towels!'

What an over-the-top PALAVER, as Molly says when everything is a mess and a bother.

I first of all took Honey and put her out in the garden again. Everyone knows (especially if you have read the excellent and informative book *Love Me, Love My Dog*) that you don't scream at a small new puppy who has just done a pee. In the book Monica Sitstill says, 'Praise the good behaviour and ignore the bad.' I think this is a glorious and marvellous way of bringing up animals *and* children to be Model Citizens and I only wish that Mum would make that her personal MOTTO when it comes to me too. If she ignored me when I got a bad report, I'm sure I wouldn't get one again, and especially I wouldn't if she praised me when I *didn't* get a bad report!

When I had cleared up the mess in the kitchen in a very efficient and effective manner I went back to the garden to get Honey and take her to her crate. She had fallen asleep on the patio. My heart grew at least three sizes in my chest (as they say in books) as I looked on MY WISH COME TRUE.

The Puppy Plan

I scooped her up into my arms and put her gently into her new bed.

'Welcome to your new home, Honey Love!' I whispered.

7

How to Behave
at the Vets'

By now Honey had spent a whole entire week at our house and had managed to stop crying at night *and* stop peeing on the floor every hour of every day. And I had spent the whole entire week (because it was half-term, so I didn't have to go to school – thank the high heavens for that) staring at Honey while she was sleeping, playing with Honey while she was awake, and staring at Honey while she was feeding. I was OVER THE TOP OF

THE MOON and HEAD OVER
HEELS in love, which generally
meant I felt quite GIDDY
most of the time.

One thing I was certainly not feeling
giddy about though was that we had to
take Honey to the vet for her injections.
In fact, I was Exceedingly Worried and
Stressed about the injections, as I cannot say
I particularly like the sight of a needle when
it is going to be used for an injection, even
if it is *not* going to be used to inject *me*. But
April was being so kind and helpful and said
she would come with me and hold my hand
and Honey's paw if necessary. All very
strange and UNCHARACTERISTIC.

'Haven't you got lots of exceedingly
important work in your office?' I asked.

'Oh well, that can wait,' said my sister
in an airy, careless sort of way. She kept

checking her reflection in the hall mirror
and turning her head
to one side and the
other and patting
her long blonde
hair. I have
always wished
so much that
I had my sister's long blonde hair. Not
actually her own hair, obviously, because
then that would make my sister bald, and
I'm not such a meany as all that. But it
would be nice to wake up one day and
have magically changed into a girl with
long blonde hair instead of being me with
short, curly auburn hair.

You know what they say:
We Blondes have all the fun!

'Why are you checking your hair so much?' I asked. 'We are only going to the vet.'

April frowned at me and then tutted as if to say, 'Honestly, you don't know anything about what it is to be a girl with long blonde hair.' But she didn't actually say anything, just grabbed Honey from me and put her in the boot of Mum's car and told me to get in too. (Not in the boot, of course.)

When we got to the vet we were actually quite early. I thought this was strange, as April never manages to be early for anything. In fact, Mum says, 'April Lydia Love, you'll be late for your own funeral,' which I think is a daft thing to say, as how can you be late when you are already dead?

The new vets' surgery was a very smart building and had one entrance for people with dogs and one for people with small pets like cats and hamsters and stick insects and things. Actually, I wonder if people really do take stick insects to the vet ever? I never did take mine. But they escaped from their jar after only two weeks of owning them, so I didn't really get the chance. Mum doesn't know they escaped. She would obviously FREAK if she knew, in case they might be living under her bed or something, which of course they might be . . .

The dog side of the building was a crazy and noisy place to be. The waiting room was full of dogs, barking and whining and trying to play with each other.

What a racket . . .
some of us are trying to
snooze, you know.

85

The Puppy Plan

Luckily for us, Honey was small enough
to sit on our laps and be held and she was
actually quite sleepy, as she always was
when we first had her. I was thinking about
the old saying that people look like their
dogs – or is it that dogs look like their
owners? – and playing a game of looking
around and trying to see if it was true. And
the people DID look like their dogs. There
was a scary kind of droopy-mouthed dog
which I think is what you call a bulldog.
He was snarling a lot and had gloops of
sticky stuff hanging from his jaws.

Someone needs to go to the
pooch parlour, methinks.

It was quite the most disgustingest kind of
beast, and I was ever so thoroughly glad
that Honey did not look like that.

Thank You so much!

Then I looked up and saw
that the man who was holding on to the
scary beast's lead was also very scary-
looking! And he had a droopy kind of face
with dribbly, gloopy bits coming out of his
mouth too. I had to look away and pretend
to examine my chewed-off nails to hide my
laughter. I didn't want the scary man and
dog to jump on me or dribble on me or
anything.

And then I looked up and saw a very
skinny dog with very short, grey silvery hair
and long dangly ears. I think it must have
been a she-dog because it was wearing a
very glistening and glimmering collar with
what I'm sure were real diamonds on it.
The famous people in the magazines Molly
brings to our Celebrity Club meetings all

have dogs with very real diamond collars
on. I wondered how much an actual real
diamond collar would cost and whether I
could maybe try to get on *Seeing Stars* and
become famous and get loads of money and
buy one for Honey.

I wouldn't say no . . .

Then I looked up and saw that dog's owner
and started feeling like I was going to laugh
all over again, because that owner was
another person who looked exactly spot-on
like her dog! The woman had long grey
hair that looked like her dog's ears and she
was even wearing an actual real diamond
necklace, which is called a choker because
it looks like it's so tight round your neck it
will actually really choke you. This time my
laughter was really getting far too difficult

and frankly uncomfortable to control and I burst out with a laugh just as the vet came out and called:

'Puppy Love – please come through!'

This sounded quite bizarre of course to everyone in the room, and they all laughed because there is an expression 'puppy love', which means that two very young people have fallen in love (I read it in one of Molly's magazines). Even though I was a bit embarrassed, I was relieved that I could let my own laughter out quite loudly now that everyone else was laughing. I thought this was quite clever of me. April obviously did not think this and grabbed me tightly by the hand, hissing, 'Shut up, Summer.'

Why on earth should I have shut up when everyone else was laughing? I can't have made April embarrassed if everyone else was laughing too. And anyway, she was using very strange and peculiar behaviour, patting her hair, snatching Honey from me and grinning at the vet in a weird daydreamy-ish way.

We went into the vet's room and April stroked Honey and put her on the table.

'Now, what can we do for your lovely new puppy, Ms Love?' asked the vet, looking straight at my sister when he was talking.

'Excuse me,' I said most politely. I wanted to correct his obvious mistake about the important fact that Honey was indeed MY lovely new puppy.

Yeah, excuse me too! First you get my name wrong, then you ignore me and talk to the girl!

'Yes, she is lovely, isn't she?' said my sister.

I thought it was very rude of her to butt in and ignore me. But I didn't say anything because I was distracted by the tone of her voice, which was all sugary and yucky-sounding and so I found myself staring at her instead. She flicked her blonde hair over her shoulders and I started dreaming again about having nice hair and thinking, 'I wish I could do that,' so I missed what the vet said back to her.

Then I looked hard at the vet and wondered how old he was. Maybe about the same age as April, sort of twenties-ish. He had nice sparkly blue eyes and a very friendly smile and a little short beard. I wish men didn't have beards. It makes it so difficult to work out how old they are, and of course it is very bad manners indeed to *ask* them how old they are, so you just have to guess. Then I thought, 'How do you eat when you have a beard? Does food get stuck in it? I wouldn't like to kiss a man with a beard. It would be so prickly, I am sure of that. But then, maybe beard-hair is soft like a puppy's? Urgh! I don't know why I thought that. *I don't like kissing*, beard or no beard!'

I suddenly realized that Honey was not happy at all. She was pulling away from the vet and whimpering.

ARGH! Have you seen the man's face? Freak out!

I snapped myself out of my dreaming and tried to calm Honey down. (It was actually a relief to be able to stop thinking about kissing men with beards.) April was holding Honey down on to the table tightly with

one hand and trying to ignore how much she was wriggling and whining, while she flicked her blonde hair around with her other hand and chatted away in that yucky voice.

'Yes, I work for Quincey and Close on the High Street,' she was saying.

How to Behave at the Vets'

Aha! So they're not actually called
Stingy and Gross . . .

But it wasn't really the moment to
check with April what her place of work
was really called as Honey was starting
to yowl and was looking at Mr Beard
in a very scared manner and trying to
back away from him off the table. I
think she had worked out about the
injection.

Forget the needle – look at
the face! Don't you think
it's weird?

I glowered in a way that I thought told my
sister to stop chatting and to let poor Honey
get her major ordeal of being injected
over and done with. April did not see the
glowering, so I put my own hand on Honey

95

and pinched my sister's hand to get her to move it from MY puppy.

'Ouch! Summer, what are you doing – *sweetie*?' said April, rubbing her hand and pretending to still smile at me while actually gritting her teeth in a threatening way.

'Sweetie?' I repeated, feeling quite baffled as she never ever calls me that. But I couldn't say any more, because Honey squirmed round and nipped *me* on the hand and then fell off the table in a howling heap.

 Hairy Face stabbed me!

'There, all done,' said Mr Beard.

I did not know what he meant, but then I saw he was holding a syringe in his hand – he was holding it up in the air in his rubber-gloved hand just like they do on

the telly in those doctor programmes and
I thought, Thank goodness, he must have
done the injection when I wasn't looking.

And then I fainted.

8

How to Behave at a Puppy Party

April was strangely cross with me
after the fainting episode at the vets',
which I thought was very Hurtful and
Uncaring and even Unsisterly of her. I said
so, but she just said that I was the Unsisterly
one and that I should know better than to
embarrass her by pinching her and fainting
in public.

Mum laughed far too long and loud
when I told her about the visit to the
vet and about how April had chatted

annoyingly to Mr Beard and not let me say
anything about MY puppy. I didn't see one
little bit what was so funny, especially since
the whole visit had been a Major Ordeal for
me and for poor little Honey.

You said it, sister.

Apparently I'd missed out on the best bit
while I'd been lying on the floor in my
dramatical fainting fit, because Mr Beard
had invited me, April and Honey to a
'puppy party' the next week! It had to be in
the evening so that people could get there
after work. This was something April was
apparently very pleased about. I was pleased
too, as I was of course at school in the day.

'I love parties!' I cried, immediately
feeling a bit better, even though I did have
an impressive lump on my head which I

kept on rubbing as I wanted Mum and April to see that I still needed lots of Tea and Sympathy. (Although I actually prefer hot chocolate and marshmallows.)

'Can Molly come? Can we dress up? Do we get to eat cake and play Pass the Parcel?' I blushed when I said that last bit, as everyone knows Pass the Parcel is a very babyish-type game, but I love it, especially when there is a jelly baby between each layer of the paper.

April did her rolly-eyed sophisticated sighing thing and said, 'No, Summer, we won't be playing silly party games. It's a party for the *puppies*, not for us. And yes, bring your little friend. It might stop you from pinching people and fainting again.'

How to Behave at a Puppy Party

I did not dignify my annoying older sister with a response to her hurtful and unsisterly comment, but rushed instead to call Molly and ask her if she wanted to come to the puppy party.

'Does the sun rise in the morning?' she asked.

So we started planning what we were going to wear (which obviously takes a week's worth of planning) and whether or not we should bring our cameras in case there were any celebrity dog owners there or maybe even teacherly Monica Sitstill, telly personality and dog trainer *extraordinaire* (that's French for fab, according to Molly who is as good at French as she is at, well, everything really).

In the end the puppy party was quite good fun, but unfortunately as it was at the

101

vets' and not at a glam Venue of any sort, there were no celebrities, just Mr Beard – although you would have thought he was a celebrity the way April spent the whole time fluttering her eyelashes and flicking her hair and crossing and uncrossing her legs. She was obviously pleased to see him again.

Honey was not.

Hey! He's hairy and he hurts puppies! Who would be pleased to see HIM?

She took one look at him when we arrived at the party and whined and hid her head in my jacket.

Molly nudged me and pointed at my sister and said, 'Do you think April's all right? She looks as if she is desperate for the loo all the time. Do you think I should tell her that there's one out in reception?'

I just said, 'No, let's concentrate on Honey.'

So we did.

Once Mr Beard had moved away from us to talk to some other people, Honey calmed down a bit and ended up having a marvellously fabulous time at the party. Apparently the whole idea about a puppy party is to get the dogs to Socialize and Interact. I worked out that this means 'get used to other dogs'. Honey is not a shy dog, I have found.

I like to work the room, you know?

She spotted the biggest dog there, which unfortunately was the huge slobbery dog with the dribble that I'd seen in the vets'

waiting room when we came for the injections, and she ran over and put her paws around his neck.

I'm not Backward in coming forward!

The big slobbery owner with the scary droopy face just stared at Honey. I tried to engage him in some polite chatty conversation about how nice it was to see our puppies playing together. It's the kind of thing I've heard Mum say to another mum when I make a new friend and go round to their house. But the scary slobbery man had obviously not mastered the art of polite chatty conversation himself, because he just stared at me like he had stared at Honey. Then his dog growled at Honey and tried to bite her.

So you like to play rough, do you?

I wanted to get her back, but Mr Beard piped up at this point and said, 'Don't worry, Autumn, that's just natural dog behaviour.'

'I'm called Summer,' I said sternly, 'and I don't like the way that dog growled at my puppy—'

'Ahem, what my little sister means is that I'm sometimes a bit overprotective of my dog,' said April, cutting in and ASTOUNDING me with her lying, which would be described as Bare-Faced, I think. In other words – OUTRAGEOUS!

'Sorry – Summer – and er . . . ?' Mr Beard looked questioningly at April, which seemed to make her face go a sort of dark red unattractively sweaty kind of colour, and she said, 'A-April,' and giggled. I was still very upset by the way she was pretending that Honey was *her* dog, so I couldn't find the words to say anything at all at this point, but it didn't matter as Mr Beard was still wittering on.

'Don't worry about the growling. It's only a little warning so that Honey doesn't get too big for her boots and play too roughly,' he said.

Molly and I exchanged a look when he said this. I knew she was thinking the same thing as me (we quite often do): how could Honey be too rough for such a horrible huge slobbery monster? I was about to say something, but Honey was actually quite happily rolling around with Slobberchops again, and anyway, Mr Beard wanted to tell us about a game called Pass the Puppy.

Aha! I thought. No 'silly party games',

eh, April? and I tried to smirk knowingly at my sister to show her that I'd been right all along, as indeed I often am.

But April was looking rather stressed and was furiously wiping at her white jeans in a quite panicky manner. Honey had bounded up to her after finishing her game with Slobberchops and had nuzzled her cute little pink nose all over April's jeans.

Just Being friendly!

Normally puppy-nuzzling is something lovely; it was just a shame that Honey had got herself totally covered in Slobberchops's slobber and was now getting April's white jeans covered in it too.

We played Pass the Puppy. (Well, Molly and I did. April didn't bother to join in as she was being what Mum calls

a Prima Donna and fussing over her jeans
and smoothing down her long blonde hair,
while she and Mr Beard nattered on about
something dull.) The game was basically
just the owners passing their puppy on to
the owner next to them, so that we all got
a chance to make a fuss of different puppies.
The puppies were supposed to get used to
being handled by different types of people.
The only thing was, the puppies were more
interested in the other puppies than in their

boring owners, so we didn't get much of chance to pat and cuddle them.

Newsflash – dogs are more interesting than people!

So we all gave up quite quickly and just let them roll around on the floor and chew each other's ears and sniff each other's bottoms which is what puppies seem to like doing more than anything.

What else is there in life?

Then at the end of the party, when the puppies were all quite worn out and exhausted, Mr Beard actually stopped talking to my sister for about five minutes and told us all about pet insurance. This was possibly the most BORING thing I have ever had to sit through in my whole long life; even more dull and deadly boring than the Victorians and their completely useless penny-farthing-type inventions.

So I started whispering with Molly about the latest programme of *Seeing Stars*, which I'd seen the night before. There had been this really lame act on which was a man who thought

he was so cool because he could ride on
a bicycle with only one wheel (which is
called a Monocle, I think) while balancing
a plate of sausages on his head and singing
'Is This the Way to Amarillo?', and he was
wearing a purple shiny suit, so honestly how
on earth he could have possibly thought he
was cool is beyond me. Also, he sang out of
tune. Also, why on earth would you want
to balance sausages? Surely he could have
come up with something more glam than
that? Of course, he didn't get many points.
And the judges were so rude! They said
to him that they would gladly show him
the way to Amarillo if only he'd take his
Monocle and ride off there right away and
take his sausages with him. It had made me
laugh till I needed the loo quite desperately.

Anyway, as I was telling Molly this
hilarious thing, I was holding Honey on

my lap. She'd gone to sleep, and she was being so quiet that I'd unfortunately sort of forgotten she was there, so when I did a marvellous and extremely realistic impression of balancing a plate of sausages on my head while wobbling on a Monocle bike, I accidentally knocked Honey and she fell off my lap at Mr Beard's feet. She woke up at once . . .

Who wouldn't, under the circumstances?

. . . and looked up to see Mr Beard bending over her to see if she was all right. Well, one look at him and Honey leaped into the air, yowling and howling and then scarpered back underneath my seat.

Hairy Needle-Man Alert!

How to Behave at a Puppy Party

This had the unfortunate effect of setting
all the other puppies off barking and
howling and they all made a dive for my
seat as well. I think they thought it was
a new party game where they had to
chase Honey.

In the confusion, I was knocked off my
seat and I bashed my head on the shelf
behind me.

And I fainted again.

9
How to Be Ahead of the Game

Mum laughed even longer and louder when I told her about how Honey had reacted to seeing Mr Beard again. Personally I thought she could have been more sensitive and caring about me Losing My Conscienceness, which is what the nurse at the vet's said my fainting had been.

'Looks like April's got a tough job on her hands,' Mum said. I thought this was a cryptical thing to say, and also frankly a stupid one — as it was *me* that got knocked out by my puppy being frightened of Mr Beard, so what did that have to do with April?

That weekend Molly came round to my house as usual. Mum and April were clattering about the kitchen and arguing about something, so we made ourselves a snack and played with Honey in what Mum still calls the Playroom, but which I call the Den, as it sounds less babyish.

While we were playing, I told Molly about this cryptical comment of Mum's, and she said she thought she had worked it out because, while I was being helped by the other vets and nurses after my second faint, Molly was watching my sister and Mr Beard talking. She secretly spied on them while pretending to put all her attention on to Honey.

Yeah, I noticed that.

Molly is very good at secretly spying on people while pretending to put all her attention on to other things. She does it at school all the time. That is how she always manages to Stay Ahead of the Game and know who is best friends with who, and

which parties everyone is going to. This is why she will make a fabulous famous journalist when she grows up so that she can report on all the celebrities we will meet when we get on the telly with our Celebrity Club.

'I have worked out all the answers to the mysteriousness of your sister's recent behaviour patterns,' Molly told me in a hushed and secretive way.

'Eh?' I said.

'I know why your sister's being weird,' Molly explained, sighing in an annoying Mum-type manner.

'Oh good,' I said. 'Does it have anything to do with Honey? Because I am feeling rather confused and upset about her pretending Honey is *her* puppy.'

Molly smirked in a way that made me realize she absolutely *did* have all the answers and was dying to let me know how clever she was. 'Well, you're on the right lines,' she said.

'Molly, just tell me,' I said in a grumpy tone. 'I am not in a mood to play guessing games of any sort.'

'It's all to do with Mr Beard!' she cried triumphantly. 'Except that is not his real name.'

'I know that!' I shouted. Then I realized I didn't actually know what his real name was. 'What is his real name then?' I asked more quietly.

Mr Beard
Veterinary
Surgeon

'It's Nick Harris,' she said smugly.

'What a boring and dull grown-up name,' I said. I was disappointed. Mr Beard was actually a much better and more DESCRIPTIVE name.

'Well, I can't do anything about that,' said Molly. She was starting to seriously annoy me now. She might be my best friend, but she can still wind me up when she wants to. Or even sometimes when she doesn't want to. 'He's called Nick Harris and he's only just become a vet because he's been a student until now, which means he's not that much older than your sister,' said Molly, still smirking.

This was not exactly an exciting piece of news that could be called a REVELATION at all.

I put on a mega-sulk, which involved me crossing my arms, rolling my eyes and saying, 'So?' in a huffy way.

'*So?*' Molly cried. '*So*, it's a very important bit of information which makes everything else fit into the picture perfectly.'

Molly was being as cryptical as Mum, and I was distinctively losing interest in this conversation. I turned to walk away, and

119

Molly realized how much I was distinctively losing interest in this conversation, so she quickly said, 'April's in love with him.'

'Argh!' I screamed. I couldn't help it. April was IN LOVE WITH HIM? This meant my sister was going to KISS A MAN WITH A BEARD!

My scream frightened Honey, who had been following me as I was about to leave the room. She jumped back and yelped.

So would you if someone trod on your tail.

Molly put her hand on my arm to calm me down. 'It's OK. I don't think *he* is in love with *her*,' she said quickly.

'Phew!' I said.

'Yet,' she said.

'What do you mean, 'yet'?' I asked.

'The thing is, Mr Be– I mean, Nick Harris, thinks Honey is April's dog doesn't he?' said Molly.

'Yes,' I said, 'and I'm very cross about—'

'I know,' said Molly, 'but listen. Nick thinks that Honey is April's new pride and joy, and it's quite obvious that Honey does not like Nick Harris, because both times she's seen him Honey has gone mad and barked and howled like a crazy thing.'

Who you calling crazy?

I thought this was quite a harsh and unkind and unsupportive thing to say about my new puppy, and was going to say so, but Molly didn't give me a chance.

'I was listening to Nick Harris and April talking, and April was saying, "Wouldn't it be lovely to go for a walk with Honey together? I would so much appreciate your professional opinion on training her," and Nick Harris said, "That would be so lovely indeed, but I don't think your dog likes me very much." And your sister kept trying other ways of saying how nice it would be to meet and Nick Harris kept talking to her in an extremely friendly way, but saying that he didn't think it would be a good idea to upset Honey while she was still so small. So he obviously does not want to go out with April, so I don't think he's in love with her *yet*.'

'Well, that's that then,' I said, feeling not a small bit relieved that Mr Beard wouldn't be going out with my sister all the time. And maybe **KISSING** her. Urgh!

How to Be Ahead of the Game

Molly was looking worried. 'I'm afraid that's not,' she said.

'That's not what?' I said, confused and bewildered.

'That's not that, I'm afraid,' she said. 'You see, if you go into the kitchen, you will find your sister sitting reading *Love Me, Love My Dog* and discussing with your mum about how to DESENSITIZE Honey to Men With Beards.'

'*What?*' I cried. 'I thought they were arguing about April running riot with Mum's credit card again.'

'They were, but they've moved on from that,' Molly said, sounding smug again. 'When I went to the loo just now I hovered invisibly by the kitchen door and listened to what they were saying. This is what journalists have to do at parties and things to get juicy Celebrity Gossip. And have

123

I got some juicy gossip for you, Summer Holly Love!'

'Yeah, yeah,' I said feeling irritated that I had not thought of this invisible hovering-in-doorways idea. 'So?'

'*So*, I heard all about how April had seen Nick Harris in town when you first got Honey and how she liked him and found out he worked in the new vets' surgery. That's why she registered Honey there in the first place.' said Molly, Warming to Her Theme. 'And it would now appear that April is very determined to get Nick Harris to go out with her – and you know that when April is very determined, she gets what she wants.'

'Yes,' I said quietly. 'But how can she make Nick Harris go out with her if he doesn't want to?' I asked. Surely not even my sister has those sorts of powers? I thought.

How to Be Ahead of the Game

Molly sighed as if I had overlooked a most obvious and basic thing. 'I heard April say to your mum that the only reason that Honey does not like Nick Harris is because he has a beard, because April has read in our book that puppies who have never seen a man with a beard before often are very scared indeed when they see such a man for the first time. And she has found in the book what she thinks is a Sensible Solution.'

'Good,' I said, thinking the book would say, 'If you care for your puppy's mental sanity, never go near men with beards ever again.'

That's my plan.

'Not good, actually,' said Molly. 'She's decided that she has to get Honey used to beards, because she *needs* Honey so that she can go and see Nick Harris again. She thinks the only way she's going to get Nick Harris to go on a date with her is if it has something to do with Honey, because that's how they met each other in the first place.'

'And how in all the earth is she planning to get Honey used to men with beards? I suppose with all your clever hovering and being invisible and everything, you will have heard that part of the conversation too!' I said grumpily.

'I did,' said Molly. 'You're not going to like this.'

'Tell me,' I demanded fiercely.

'She's going to do what Monica Sitstill advises in the book. She is going to buy some false beards and get us all to wear them.'

ME, WEAR A BEARD?

I nearly almost fainted again.

10
How to Fight Like
Cat and Dog

Luckily the beard-buying trip idea was not mentioned when Mum and April came out to say goodbye to Molly when it was time for her to go home. I decided that I did not want to hang around the house in case April *did* mention a beard-buying trip, so I went out into the garden to play with Honey. At least she was sane and normal. Or so I thought.

Actually Honey started doing something really strange with Cheese and Toast. She

was creeping towards them on her belly and twitching her head to one side. I thought at first maybe she was ill. I had never seen her move like that before. Cheese and Toast were sitting staring at her, and you could tell they were also thinking this was strange. They were most probably thinking, 'Who is this bizarre creature?'

Who are you calling Bizarre?

How to Fight Like Cat and Dog

Cats always look as if they are thinking this, whoever they are looking at. This is because cats think everyone except another cat is a weird creature. They are HAUGHTY and ALOOF – that's what Molly's mum, Mrs Cook, says. Mrs Cook does not like cats.

Honey then jumped towards Cheese and Toast, and of course they hissed at her and scratched her. They are always hissing and scratching. They even hiss and scratch at *each other*. They used to be good friends when they were kittens, but now they ignore each other or fight. I suppose that's what sisters do in real true human life, so why should cats be any different? Anyway, Honey was frankly very upset by this behaviour. In fact she yelped, as Cheese and Toast have very sharp claws.

Not very friendly, these puppies . . .

But whereas I would most definitely never go near Cheese and Toast again if they scratched me, Honey crept nearer them on her belly again.

These puppies are funny little guys. Why won't they play?

Cheese and Toast looked really very miffed that Honey was not getting their message, and so Cheese pounced on Honey. Honey did not get this message either; she seemed to think it was a message that said, 'Let's play,' but in cat language it of course meant the total opposite of that.

I've told them I'm a nice friendly pooch. But they are just not on my wavelength . . .

So Honey got scratched again. I decided I should call Mum to come outside as I was getting a bit anxious that Honey might get really hurt, and of course I was not really in the mood for taking her to the vet if she got injured, because I didn't want to see Mr Be– Harris again.

'Mum! Come and see what's going on with Honey and Cheese and Toast!' I shouted.

Mum came out. 'What's the matter?' she asked.

'I'm worried Honey's going to get hurt,' I explained worriedly. 'What can I do? Cheese and Toast keep scratching at her to get her to keep away from them, but Honey

131

keeps trying to get closer to them. It doesn't make any kind of sense. She is basically not getting their message.'

Mum watched the three animals rolling around and crouching and pouncing and then burst out laughing.

'Honey, you daft mutt!' she cried.

Who me?

Honey had stopped rolling around with the cats for a moments and was looking up at me with her head on one side — what if she understood?

'Look, Summer,' said Mum, 'Cheese and Toast speak a completely different language from Honey.'

It would seem so.

I did not understand this. Animals do not speak. Unless maybe my mum had hidden talents like Doctor Dolittle and she could speak to the animals? I was pondering over this particularly strange idea when I realized Mum was still talking to me – in human language.

'The cats lie flat when they are going to pounce and attack something – you've seen them do that when they are trying to catch a bird, haven't you?'

'Yes – so what?'

'Well, when Honey lies flat she's trying to tell the cats that she won't hurt them, she's just being friendly. It's called being submissive,' Mum explained.

That's right. But these little puppies just don't get it!

133

'I doubt Honey even realizes that Cheese
and Toast are cats,' Mum continued. 'Frank
didn't have any cats at his house, did he?'
I shook my head. 'She probably thinks
Cheese and Toast are puppies like her, and
she's trying to work out how to play with
them. I've been reading your *Love Me, Love
My Dog* book with April – there's loads of
interesting stuff in there about how new
puppies relate to pets that are already in the
family,' said Mum.

Yeah, I thought, there's loads of
interesting stuff in there about how new
puppies relate to beards too. But I didn't say
anything as I was trying hard not to think
about my sister kissing beardy guys, and
anyway, Mum was sounding very pleased
with her knowledgableness
on the subject of puppies
for the first time since

we had got Honey, so I didn't want to interrupt.

'I think the only thing we can do about Cheese and Toast is let them sort things out with Honey in their own way. She'll get the message eventually.'

I nodded, but secretly did not think this was a very likely thing, as I watched Honey trying to shake both cats off her back while they held on like their claws were superglued into her fur.

I am beginning to get seriously worried that Mum might in fact be right and that my dog might be one dog biscuit short of a full barrel – in other words, daft.

DAFT? ME? Humph.

11
How to Desensitize Your Puppy

My sister, April Lydia Love, had just **INSULTED** me.

'You and your little friend have been spying on me!' she was yelling. It was not an attractive way to behave, I thought, as it made her face go a tomatoey-ketchupy kind of colour.

'What do you actually mean by

"spying"?' I said in a cool and calm way. (I was doing what Molly calls PLAYING FOR TIME, which is when you know you've been caught out, but you don't want to have to admit it straight away as you are hoping there might be a way out of the Difficult Situation you have found yourself in.)

'YOU KNOW WHAT "SPYING" MEANS!' shrieked April in a scarily dramatical manner, flicking her hair around quite fiercesomely and huffing like a steam train.

If only Nick could see you now, I thought, a little bit meanly.

'I HEARD MOLLY TELL YOU ABOUT ME FANCYING NICK AND ABOUT HIS BEARD AND EVERYTHING!' April was really quite shouting by this point.

'Oh,' I said.

That was all I could manage to say. I was actually suddenly speechless with shock that my only sister could stoop so incredibly low as to spy on me and my best friend having a private conversation. (Even though I suppose Molly *had* been spying on *her* before. But then, April is older than us and really should know better.)

'So, *Summer*,' April said, in less of a shouty way (more of an 'I'm your older sister, so you'd better listen up' tone of speaking), 'the cat really is out of the bag now. And to make it up to me, you and your little friend are going to come shopping with me for beards.'

'WHAT?' I almost nearly choked to death right there on the very spot. 'You want us to go and buy a false beard together – and you've been keeping the cats in a bag as *well*?' I wailed at my sister. How much more mad could a person get? If this was what love did to you, I for one was NEVER going to fall in it . . .

'Are you really that stupid, or do you just enjoy winding me up?' April asked.

I didn't think I would dignify that extremely rude and unnecessary question with a grown-up response.

I rang Molly and asked her if she would come with me for this humiliating experience. Of course she said yes, but I didn't think it was because she wanted to support me. Secretly I thought she was doing it to get a bit of a laugh and to collect valuable material for future articles she would write about her childhood life when she was eventually famous. Or maybe she wasn't interested in becoming famous any more. We had not had much time to do our Celebrity Club recently, what with all the puppy stuff and spying on my sister and now going on a shopping trip for beards.

April drove us into town in Mum's car as I said I absolutely did not want to be seen walking back from town carrying a bag of beards and that we would have to put them in the boot. April did at least see the sensibleness of this suggestion.

We went to a shop called Dressed to Thrill. It was advertised as a theatrical supplies shop, but actually in true life it was more of a fancy-dress shop, where everyone went when they wanted to get an outfit for a party or a school show or something. It was not really a proper theatrical sort of place where celebrities go. The costumes were all shiny and quite unreal and didn't look at all how proper nurses/queens/

140

firemen/Robin Hoods would dress. It was
never very convincing when you got a
costume from there. I knew this because I
had to go there with Mum for parties and
things. I never really felt In Character like
a real actor would when I was dressed in
something from there. Once I went to a
party dressed as Cinderella and the rags
from the dress kept falling off and I had to
stick them back on again with bits
of chewing gum as that was
all I had with me at the time.

I think if you were in a play
and you wanted to look like a true-life
King Henry the Eighth, for example, you
would have to write to the BBC and ask
them for a costume, because they are the
only ones who really know what a true-life
King Henry the Eighth would look like. He
most certainly would not wear shiny clothes

made from nylon and plastic, which is all you get from Dressed to Thrill. I don't even know why it's called Dressed to Thrill, as I have never been thrilled in any way about anything I have ever seen in there.

So you can see why I was not at all sure that we would even find a beard in the shop that would look like a true-life beard. In fact, I was quite hopeful we would not.

In any case, the man who ran the shop was 'the looniest of loony tunes on Radio Loony', to quote Molly, and I was not looking forward to having to talk to him.

'Hello, luvvies!' he cried as soon as we entered his totally dodgy ESTABLISHMENT. The bell on the door played the first few bars of one of the songs from Disney's *Beauty and the Beast*, which I found very annoying and showy-offy, and actually somewhat childish.

'Now, luvvies, what are we after today?' the man asked. He was dressed in an OUTLANDISH and frankly embarrassing-to-look-at outfit of a piratical nature. He had a huge white blouse instead of a normal man's shirt and wore those big pirate-ish boots over black trousers. And he had a twirly black moustache, which I know wasn't real as it wasn't on straight. It didn't bode well for the beards.

'Hello,' said April in her businesslike work voice that she uses if ever you call her in the office at Stingy and Gross or whatever it's called. 'We've come to buy some beards.'

'Aha! In a lovely play together, are you, luvvies? One of those fabulous Shakespearian ones where the ladies get to dress up as men?' he chortled in an overenthusiastic way, as if he got an immense amount of pleasure from selling beards to people on a daily basis.

'Y-yes,' stammered April. I was shocked that she was doing another one of her Bare-Faced Lies, but then I supposed she couldn't really tell him the truth, which was of course: 'No, we are desensitizing our puppy to men with beards, as I have fallen in love with a vet with a beard but the puppy doesn't like him.'

'*Lovely*, luvvies!' cried the man, and he threw his arms up in the air in a very over-the-top dramatical gesture, which made his moustache detach itself completely on one side and nearly come off. He didn't seem to notice though and swung round to face the rest of the shop, calling out to us to follow him to the Facial Hair section.

We spent the next hour trying on various different colours and shapes and sizes of beard. April was very fussy and critical the whole time and got exceedingly impatient with me and Molly when we had rather a long giggling session. I have found it is honestly very difficult not to have a rather long giggling session while trying on beards.

In the end we did find three small beards that were sort of like the one that Nick Harris had, and we paid for them and put them in a bag and hurried back to the car.

When we got home, April made us put the beards on in the car.

I was very dead set against this. 'I'll

145

put mine on inside,' I said firmly. 'What if someone from school saw me wearing a beard? I would never live it down if I was known at school as the Bearded Lady or Beardy Weirdy or something cruel and unkind like that.'

'No,' said April, even more firmly, 'it's very important that Honey sees us with the beards as soon as we walk through the door. We'll just confuse her if we go into the kitchen looking normal and then put the beards on in front of her.'

'Heavens above forbid that we should look *normal*,' muttered Molly in the sort of tone her mum uses when she is getting impatient with Molly's dad about something, which is quite often.

I thought I might start a long giggling session again, but then I caught the look on my sister's face – it was a very determined and angry look – and I thought perhaps another long giggling session was not a good idea just at that moment.

We put on our beards and scurried around to the back entrance of the house so that no one would see us. We went in

through the kitchen and there was cute
little Honey, sitting in her crate, waiting
for us to come back. Unfortunately as soon
as she saw us she went BANANAS-
DOOLALLY-CRAZY, barking like she'd
gone totally mad, and started trying to eat
her way out of the crate.

Smell's Bells! Who are
these hairy guys?

'Quick!' said April. 'Back out again!'

We went back out.

'What are you doing?' I asked. 'I
thought you wanted us to go in with our
beards on?'

'I do, but we have to keep coming in
and going out until she *doesn't* bark when
she sees us come in,' said April. Talk about
confusing – and to think I'd been worried

about *Honey* getting muddled. 'The minute she sees us with beards and *doesn't* bark, we let her out of the crate and give her a big hug and a treat,' April continued.

This sounded loop-the-loop to me.

'It's what it says in *Love Me, Love My Dog*,' said April. 'It says, "Your puppy has to realize that Good Things happen around men with beards."'

Molly sniggered. 'That's what you're hoping, isn't it, April?'

April glowered. At least I think she did. It was a bit difficult to see behind the beard.

So we spent what felt like hours going in and out of the house trying to get Honey used to the beards. Eventually we had to stop because we were all getting hot and

sweaty in our facial hair, and I told April
that I thought Honey needed to get out
of her crate and go to the loo in the
garden.

Forget the loo –
I JUST WANT OUT!

April went off in a huffy mood into the
sitting room, still wearing her beard. Perhaps
wearing it made her feel closer to Nick
Harris, like she was already KISSING HIS
BEARD or something. URGH! She turned
on the telly and flopped crossly down on to
the sofa.

I angrily shoved my beard into the bag
we'd brought it home in and took
poor Honey outside. She immediately
calmed down and jumped up to lick
my face.

HeY, You're Back! You should have seen these hairy guys that kept coming in and out while you were away . . .

'The things you do for love, eh?' said Molly, pulling off her beard as well and following us out to the garden.

'Humph,' I muttered. I was truly miffed and embarrassed by this whole palaver and determined not to do this beard-desensitizing thing ever again. 'What are we going to do, Molly? We have to get April to stop wanting to use Honey to get to Nick Harris. Honey is *my* puppy. Why should April get away with upsetting her like this? I don't care if Honey doesn't like beards! I don't like them either. I wish Mum would tell April to sort out her Romantic Problem on her own and leave me and Honey out of it.'

Molly nodded. Then she laughed.

'Why are you laughing?' I cried in an exasperated tone. 'You are my Best Friend. Best Friends do not laugh in times of crisis like this one. You should be helping me.'

'I know – that's why I laughed. I have had an idea,' she said. 'Listen, what if we put Nick Harris off your sister once and for all so that he absolutely definitely totally does not want to go out with her?'

Now this was possibly quite an unkind thing to do, and probably definitely unsisterly. I thought about it for a split moment and then said, 'OK. What do you have in mind?'

Molly told me her Masterly Plan.

And I laughed too.

12
How to Desensitize Your Vet

Molly persuaded me to put her Masterly Plan into operation straight away while my extremely annoying and embarrassing older sister was watching telly. I agreed at once in case I thought about it too much and decided to change my mind.

Molly used the kitchen phone to ring the vets' surgery.

'Hello, may I please speak with Mr Nicholas Harris the vet, please,' she said. She put on a posh telephone voice which was extremely EFFECTIVE and made her sound older and definitely maturer. 'Oh, he's out making house calls? Actually, would it be possible to contact him and ask him to make a house call here to my particular place of abode?' Molly was possibly slightly overdoing the posh telephone voice, but I thought she must know what she was doing. 'Thank you so much. It's my puppy you see – Honey. Yes, Honey Love, that's the one. She's ever so poorly and really I can't see how I would get her in the car . . . so Mr Harris will be here shortly? Thank you so much. My name? Yes, certainly. It's April Love.'

I was quite a little bit SHOCKED by this lie of Molly's, which was really as Bare-Faced as the ones my sister had been telling about being the owner of Honey instead of me, but it had to be part of the plan to make sure that Nick did actually get here while April was still watching telly. I crept into the sitting room to check that April was indeed still there, and she'd actually fallen asleep in front of an old black-and-white film, and was still wearing her beard!

Molly and I sat in the kitchen with Honey and waited for the Masterly Plan to take effect. We decided to pass the time by doing a bit of training with Honey. I had not really done much of this up to this point, as Honey was still so tiny.

We flicked through the *Love Me, Love My Dog* book until we found the section on training. It was very useful as the author, Monica Sitstill, had divided all the different training commands up into little sections so that you could easily find the bit on 'How to Make Your Dog Sit' or 'How to Make Your Dog Stay' and so on, etc.

The Puppy Plan

'Let's try and get Honey to understand the "sit" command first,' said Molly. She always takes charge when we are together, and sometimes I find this annoying, but this time she was doing me an extremely Good Deed by helping me with her Masterly Plan, so I decided I wouldn't find it annoying this time.

'I'll get some of the treats we bought her,' I said as Molly read aloud from the book about what we had to do.

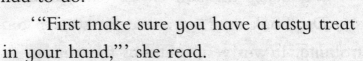

'"First make sure you have a tasty treat in your hand,"' she read.

'Check!' I said. I like using that word like that, because it is what they say on those programmes when people are in aeroplanes and are checking important items off a list before they go on a secret mission.

'"Call your dog,"' Molly went on.

'Honey!' I called.

Honey was already lying at my feet, so she couldn't come to me. She put her head on one side, but didn't get up or anything.

Why call me? I'm here already.

Molly read out the next bit: '"Show your dog the treat. Let him [or her, of course] sniff it, but don't let him [or her] eat it."'

Ha! Easier said than done. The minute I showed Honey the treat, she snatched it and gobbled it up.

Yum! Snack time!

Molly sighed and said, 'Get another treat and try again. This time, wait till Honey's

157

standing up and then hold the treat just above her nose so that she has to tip her head back to look at it. Monica Sitstill says that this will make the dog sit and then you can say "sit" and give Honey the treat the moment she sits.'

I tried again. Honey was standing now and watching the biscuit with a beady, greedy look in her eye. I held the biscuit above Honey's head. She jumped up and snatched it again before I could say anything at all.

This is my kinda game!

I was starting to get quite fed up with Honey. And Molly was starting to get quite fed up with me.

'You're not concentrating, Summer,' she said in her bossy voice, which always makes me feel like I don't want to carry on playing with her any more. I did my best to take a deep breath and Not React, which is what Mum is always advising me to do when April annoys me.

I took another treat and held it over Honey's head again, but this time I held on to it very tightly as there was absolutely no way I was going to let her snatch it. She looked at the biscuit and I moved it a bit further back over her head so that she had to tip her head back like it said in the book. I said 'sit!' and she sat!

I fed her the treat, then Molly and I whooped and jumped around and said, 'Good dog! Good dog, Honey!'

Look at you, leaping about all over the place. I only sat down. You guys get excited over the weirdest things . . .

159

But, hey, you want to jump and whoop now? OK, I'm up for a bit of jumping and whooping!

Honey started jumping and whooping too – well, yapping anyway, and we were having so much fun we nearly didn't hear the front doorbell ring.

But luckily we heard it just in time and luckily April heard it too and woke up with a start and ran to answer the door, which was all part of Molly's Masterly Plan.

'Oh, er, hello,' said a voice, which was most definitely Nick Harris's beardy voice.

'Hi!' said April. We were spying on her from behind the kitchen door. She was doing the hair-flicking thing, which obviously meant she was pleased to see him.

'Erm, I got a call to say that Honey
was ill,' said Nick Harris.

Me? Ill? I've never felt better!
The Blonde with the Beard's not
looking too hot though . . .

Nick was talking in a hesitant sort of
manner and looking at my sister in a funny
way, and it was no wonder because she was
STILL WEARING THE BEARD!

But of course, she had not realized that she was. Molly and I were trying very hard indeed not to have one of our giggling sessions. I leaned a bit further out of the kitchen so that I could get a good view of what was happening at the front door.

'Oh, I don't think so,' said April, and then she said, 'but why don't you come in and have a cup of tea?'

'N-no, I won't, actually,' said Nick Harris, holding his hand out in front of him and backing off down the driveway as if my sister was a dangerous animal he was trying to get away from very quickly indeed.

'Oh, OK, if you're sure?' said my sister, flicking her hair in a quite desperate manner.

'Yes – thanks – I'm sure!' Nick Harris shouted and he broke into a run as he got closer to his car. He fumbled with the keys and dropped them. He did look really quite panicky, and although it was funny and Molly's Masterly Plan had obviously worked in a truly masterful way, I did begin to feel a little bit guilty that Nick Harris was looking so freaked.

April shrugged and closed the door. As she did so, she caught sight of her reflection in the mirror and saw . . . THE BEARD!

'Oh, Argh! EEEEEK! OH NOOOOO!' she cried. Then very unfortunately for us, Molly and I could not hold in our giggling any longer and some giggles spilt out and April heard us.

She turned on her heel, ripping the beard off her face as she did so and bellowed in an extremely loud voice:

'YOU'LL REGRET THIS, SUMMER HOLLY LOVE – YOU MARK MY WORDS!'

She actually looked a bit like a cross between Monica Sitstill and Mr Elgin and I was actually quite scared.

Molly was still giggling behind the door though and whispered, 'I don't think we'll be seeing any more of Mr Nick Harris – or his beard! One vet well and truly desensitized.'

No more Mr Hairy Guy!

13
How to Find Your Puppy Love

April told Mum about the Beard Episode later that day. I could tell that Mum wanted badly to laugh long and loud about it, but she could obviously tell that April very much did *not* want her to, so Mum did not. But her mouth twitched a lot at the corners, and her face went quite beetrooty.

April stormed up to her room and said she was going back to work the next day as it would be more of a holiday than being at home with me in This Madhouse. She also told Mum that we should never have got Honey because she was a Liability. She said that I would never make a good dog owner because I didn't care about Honey's behaviour and that we would all 'Live To Regret The Day That Mutt Ever Set Foot In This House'.

 Who's she calling 'Mutt'?

All this was so unfair, because the only thing Honey had done wrong so far was not like a man with a beard that my sister happened to be in love with.

When April had gone to work the next morning, I told Mum this.

Mum said, 'I know that your sister is being unfair, not to mention a little strange, but that's what being in love does to people, I'm afraid.'

I said that in that case there was no way in the history of the world, or indeed the universe, that I would ever fall in love with anyone. *Ever.*

Mum smiled and gave me a hug. 'You love Honey though, don't you?' she said.

'Don't be daft, Mum. That is *no way* the same thing,' I said, rolling my eyes. Honestly, Mum is on such a different wavelength most of the time I wonder how she ever manages to cope out there in the Big Wide World.

'Of course, Summer. I know that,' said Mum. 'But I was just thinking, well, maybe April's just a bit upset because you've got Honey and you're really happy about that, but she can't seem to get Nick interested in her and *she's* really unhappy about *that*. So maybe you should help her.'

I didn't understand this at all. 'Mum,

if Nick Harris doesn't like April, there's nothing *I* can do about it,' I explained patiently.

Mum smiled again. 'Wouldn't you like it if April stopped trying to come between you and Honey?' she asked, sounding almost as patient as I did.

'Hmm,' I replied. I didn't know what Mum was up to, and I didn't want to be too enthusiasticated in case it was something dodgy.

'Well, I have a theory,' Mum went on, her eyes twinkling with mischief in a very un-Mum-like way. 'If we can engineer things so that Nick and April get together for a date, I think I can guarantee that April will lose interest in Honey overnight.'

I pulled the face that Molly calls my Dubious Expression, which is when I turn down the corners of my mouth and raise my eyebrows to show that I am unsure about an idea. Still, maybe Mum had a point. Maybe if April got together with the love of her life, I would be left in peace and quiet with the love of mine – that is, Honey.

'OK,' I said. 'But how are we going to engineer things like that?'

Mum grinned. 'First we need to arrange for Nick and April to bump into each other without Honey being there,' said Mum. Her eyes looked a bit crafty now and less twinkly. 'I think I can organize something,' she continued, 'but you've got to keep shtum,' she added, which I guessed must be Mum's way of saying it would be a secret from April.

She went on to unfold her Masterly Plan. Honestly, everyone seemed to be having Masterly Plans apart from me. I just had to cross my fingers and toes and hope to high heavens above that this one would work . . .

That evening, Mum put one of her most delicious-looking lasagnes in the oven. On the

dot of six o'clock April walked through the door. Her lasagne-radar-smell-o-vision was obviously working.

Mm-hmmm! She's not alone there.

'Nice day, dear?' asked Mum.

'Yeah, great to be out of this madhouse,' said April. 'Is it lasagne for tea?'

'Yes, but unfortunately Summer and I won't be able to stay and have it with you,' said Mum.

'Oh?' I could tell April was still very miffed with me and Mum and the Whole World in General as she often is when only one person has upset her and she decides to let everyone in the nearby VICINITY know about it.

'Yes, er, Summer and I have decided to go to the town hall this evening to a new dog-training class that we've only just found out about,' Mum said. I didn't think she sounded like she was being very convincing or truthful, but April didn't seem to notice. 'We'll be out for a couple of hours – with

Honey too, of course,' she added. Then she beckoned to me, grabbed the dog lead and her coat and, taking me by the hand, she almost ran out of the house.

'Don't bother saving us any lasagne!' Mum called as we ran to the car with Honey. 'We'll grab something in town.'

Hey! Don't listen to her! That lasagne had my name on it.

I wondered whether April would think it was odd that Mum had laid two places for tea.

Mum and I went to the park and played a bit with Honey. She'd packed us some sandwiches so we ate them while Honey chased butterflies and bees and made us laugh.

You guys are easy to please!

After a while Mum said she thought it would be fine to go home, so we did. I was hoping that April would be in a better mood now that she had had the house to herself for a bit and that there was lasagne for tea.

As it turned out, she was in a much better mood, but I don't think it had much to do with the lasagne.

When Mum and I walked into the kitchen, April was still sitting at the table. She had a man with her who I didn't recognize. I was rather a bit perplexed as this man definitely wasn't Nick. What was my strange sister up to now? Had she just gone and wrecked Mum's Masterly Plan by falling in love with a different person?

Then April looked up and said, 'Hello!'

173

The man turned round and said, 'Hello!' too, and I thought, I recognize that voice, but I still don't recognize the face.

'You don't recognize me, do you, Summer?' said the man.

Then I realized – and I nearly fainted, which would have meant I was beginning to make a habit of it, so I'm very extremely glad I did not.

It was Nick Harris!

With no beard!

Honey rushed over to him and licked his hand.

'That's better,' said Nick. 'You like me now, don't you?'

NO idea who you are, But you sure smell good!

April was blushing very much indeed, and Mum was smiling a lot.

'Why haven't you got a beard?' I asked. 'Was this part of your plan, Mum?'

'Summer!' she hissed.

'What plan?' asked April.

'Nothing,' said Mum and started to rummage about in the cupboard as if she was looking for something very important and simply didn't have time to answer any questions.

Nick laughed. 'No, Summer, your mum didn't have anything to do with me shaving off my beard! I just realized that it was – how shall I put it? – coming in between me and someone I quite liked.'

He was patting Honey's head as he spoke so I asked, 'What, you mean, you and Honey?' I felt quite a bit panicky and I hoped he was not going to take my beautiful puppy away from me.

'NO! Well, not really,' Nick answered. 'I wanted to see your sister again, but I could tell that Honey wasn't going to let me near her as long as I kept my beard. It's quite common for new puppies not to like men with beards.'

I had a sudden thought. 'Mum, did you *tell* Nick why we bought the beards?' I asked.

April did not seem to appreciate me mentioning the Beard Episode again. She jumped up, knocking the rest of the lasagne on to the floor.

At last – the moment I've been waiting for!

'Don't worry, April,' said Nick. 'If it wasn't for your mum, I wouldn't be here tonight.'

176

How to Find Your Puppy Love

April was speechless, which I think is the very first time in her life since I have known her that she has been.

Nick explained that Mum had called to say that Honey was ill and that this time it was real and could he please come round after six o'clock to see her. Nick had of course said yes, because he is a very professional and caring vet who loves dogs, even dogs who don't like him and who live in houses with Bearded Ladies.

He had turned up to find that Honey wasn't there – only April, who invited him in to apologize about the Beard Episode, and they had ended up eating the lasagne together, which is of course exactly what Mum had wanted them to do. They had had a lovely evening and had agreed to see each other again at the weekend. April started blushing again when Nick said this last bit.

'But I still don't understand why you don't have a beard any more?' I said.

Nick blushed this time, and because he didn't have a beard any more, you could see all of the blush.

'I shaved it off,' he said.

'Well obviously,' I said. 'But why?'

'Because I didn't want April's puppy to freak out at me,' he explained. 'After I saw April wearing a false beard, I thought about why a beautiful girl would go around wearing a beard and then I remembered that Honey had got really upset both times she had seen me at the surgery, so I thought maybe April was trying to get Honey used to seeing a beard. Some of those dog books suggest it as a way of desensitizing your dog,' he added. 'So I thought, April won't bring Honey to see me again if Honey doesn't get used to beards, and if April doesn't bring her puppy to see me, I won't get to see April . . . And so, I shaved off my beard.'

By this time, Nick and April were both grinning and blushing so much they looked like a pair of CERTIFIABLE lunatics and I felt like I wanted to just turn around and leave them both to it. Then I suddenly realized what an AWFUL MISTAKE Nick Harris had just made. I had to put him straight once and for all before disaster struck . . .

'Honey is MY puppy, not April's!' I cried.

Yeah – you're the mummy!

'Oh,' said Nick Harris.

'Yes,' I said in a firm and stern tone, 'April only *pretended* Honey was hers so that she could get to meet you properly after she saw you in town and liked you and found out where you worked.'

Mum stepped in to De-Fuse the Tension at this point, except she obviously couldn't think of a funny jokey way to do it so she just said, 'All's well that ends well,' which was pretty lame, I thought. 'Nick and April are together, and April will leave you and Honey to it from now on, I'm sure,' Mum added.

Luckily Nick seemed to think that Mum had actually told a hilarious joke anyway – either that or he was good at playing along at the whole De-Fusing the Tension idea – so he laughed. And then April laughed. And then, bizarrely, I started to see the funny side of the whole embarrassing Beard-Puppy-Confusion-Love-Story thing, and I laughed too.

Since that very day, Nick and April have

continued to be NAUSEATINGLY loved-up. And this is very fine by me, as Honey is now totally and absolutely

MY pUppY again,

and I must admit that I am quite loved-up with her too. Although not nauseatingly so. At least, I don't think so. And Molly comes round all the time and is Second-in-Command with everything to do with Honey. Even though I know she would prefer to be First-in-Command.

So that's the story of how my wish came true and I got my Puppy Love and how my sister nearly wrecked my wish by claiming my puppy as her own while behaving totally weirdly and frankly mega-embarrassingly . . . But how she, in the end, got her love too!

Don't you just love
a happy ending?

Collect them all!

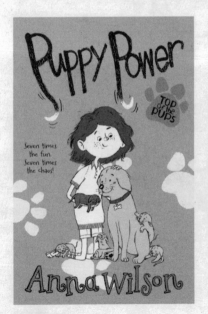